This Book Belongs To

_____

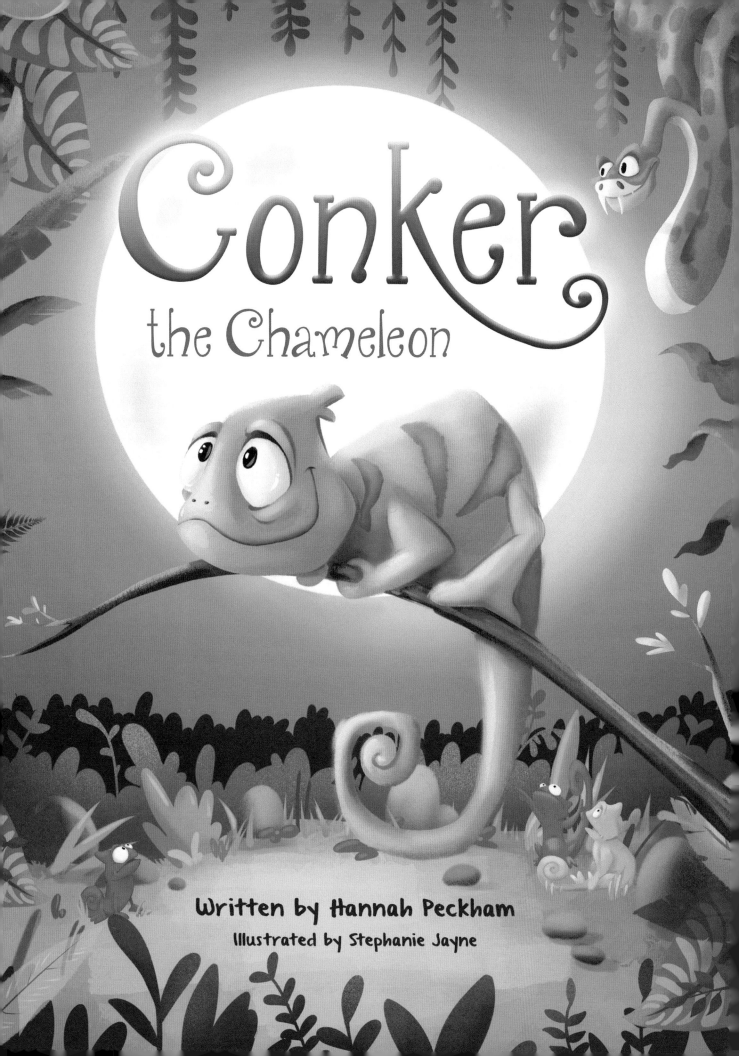

To my dearest daddy
up on the naughty cloud,
my beloved son Bodhi
who is the centre of my universe,
and my mum,
without whom I could not have done it.

Published in the United Kingdom by:

Blue Falcon Publishing
The Mill, Pury Hill Business Park,
Alderton Road, Towcester
Northamptonshire NN12 7LS
Email: books@bluefalconpublishing.co.uk
Web: www.bluefalconpublishing.co.uk

A CIP record of this book is available from the British Library.

First printed February 2021
ISBN 9781912765294

Conker
the Chameleon

Hannah Peckham

Conker the chameleon
was just like all the others.
There wasn't that much difference
between him and all his brothers.

From when he hatched the likenesses
were there for all to see.
His sticky tongue and curly tail
matched almost perfectly.

But something niggled at him
as he watched the hatchlings play.
There was one thing quite different –
maybe it would change one day?
Yet as the weeks went by,
Conker grew sadder and seemed duller,
And soon the others noticed, too...

...he

could

not

change

his

colour.

Now humans tend to think
this special colour change takes place,
So chameleons can hide if their enemies give chase.
And yet this isn't true
(and what's the harm in me revealing).
In fact, it's all about what chameleons are feeling.

They turn a vivid yellow

And a happy shade
of green,

Blue is for their sadness,
like rough waves

And red is
angry, raging
bright,

if fearfulness is present,

which is really rather pleasant.

on stormy oceans,

uncomfortable. emotions.

Over time their words were lost
and the colours took their place.
The need to talk and listen just
seemed gone without a trace.

Eventually, their colour
was the only way to tell,
How chameleons were feeling,
but it didn't work that well.

Conker tried his hardest,
but his difference made him muddled.
A big fat tear rolled down his face
as he was feeling troubled.

Yet on this morning, Conker
(a determined little chap),
Resisted the temptation to
extend his morning nap.

Instead, quite out of nowhere
(just as these things often do),
an idea popped into his head,
and he shouted, "Woohoo!"

Chameleons can shed their skin.
You see, it's very clever.
They grow so fast it doesn't fit
and comes off altogether.

If they had no use for what was shed,
bright blue and red and green,
A recycled coat of colours
would make his feelings seen.
He would no longer feel alone
and they would understand,
Whatever he was going through
and lend a helping hand.

In all of the excitement and,
of course, now wide awake,
Conker fell into the path
of Sam, a hungry snake!
As you have learned, chameleons
turn yellow out of fright,
But Conker's dull skin went unseen,
as snakes have bad eyesight.

Conker grabbed his chance,
escaping easily with glee.
He'd avoided being lunch because
snakes can't really see!

He carried on his journey, slightly shaken from the fright.
Then saw two red chameleons having the loudest fight.
Conker stopped to listen to what each of them had said,
But their fight made him confused, so he stopped to scratch his head.

As he heard the two friends argue, an idea began to glisten.
These pals would only fix the rift if they could stop and listen.
"Now you look here!" he shouted - he felt bold on this occasion -

"It seems to me you've clearly had
a miscommunication."

So the two friends listened well
to what the other had to say,
And with that Conker's job was done,
and he went on his way.

Conker's coat would need some blue
for him to show his sorrow,
Yet tired from his day he thought he'd leave it 'til tomorrow.

Just then, he spotted something
from the corner of his eye.
It was a blue chameleon
who seemed about to cry.

He waited for a moment as he hoped not to intrude,
Then cleared his throat and spoke the words,

"I hope this isn't rude.
I noticed you looked very glum
there, sitting by yourself.
But talking about how you feel
can help your mental health."

So they shared some of their worries,
not the easiest thing to do,
Yet sat in peaceful friendship,
with a little sniff from Blue.
And they slowly came to realise
guessing feelings every day,
Based on someone else's colour
was not really the best way.

Then they noticed that by talking,
their sadness had now shifted.
The cloud that hung there just before
it seemed had somehow lifted.
Saying how you feel inside,
is not all that hard really.
Just talk to someone that you trust
who cares about you dearly.

Conker was excited to have
made another friend,
And walked back to his branch
now that the day was at an end.
He climbed his tree as quickly as
his tired feet would allow,
A little smile upon his face,
for things seemed different now.

Although his world was
just the same as it
had been before,
Something inside
himself had changed,
he thought,
then thought some
more.

Not turning vivid
yellow had just saved
him from the snake.
He'd also helped two
friends to overcome
their big mistake.

And surely a recycled coat
might seem a little bonkers,
His own skin may be different
but at least it was all Conker's.

Guessing mood is tricky,
so a coat just wouldn't do.
He had to tell them how he felt,
so everybody knew.
He drifted off to sleep not knowing
what may lie ahead,
Yes, he still couldn't change colour,
but he could use words instead.

And with that twinkling of a thought,

his eyes closed dreamily,

And he whispered to himself,

"It's pretty awesome...

...being me!"

Self-care scavenger hunt

Find your favourite toy.

Hug someone you love.

Find something that is your favourite colour.

Write down something nice someone has said about you (or just remember what they said).

Find something soft that's nice to touch.

Play/sing a song that you like to sing/dance to.

Tell someone something good about themself.

Find something that comes from nature.

Find something that makes you smile.

Draw a picture of your favourite memory and remember what made it special and how you felt.

My ChaMEleon tree

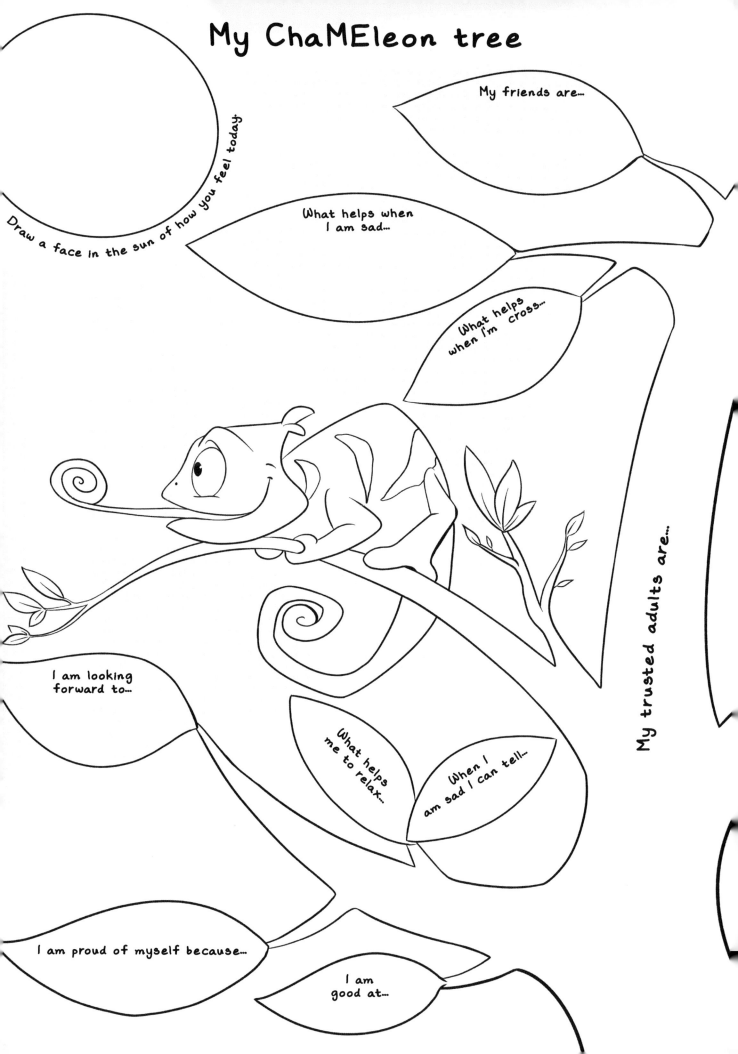

Draw a face in the sun of how you feel today.

My friends are...

What helps when I am sad...

What helps when I'm cross...

My trusted adults are...

I am looking forward to...

What helps me to relax...

When I am sad I can tell...

I am proud of myself because...

I am good at...

Printed in Great Britain
by Amazon